Hazel Hutchins

# Robyn's Want Ad

Illustrations by Yvonne Cathcart

FIRST NOVELS

The New Series

D1047996

Formac Publishing Limited
Halifax, Nova Scotia

The development and pre-publication work on this project was funded in part by the Canada/Nova Scotia Cooperation Agreement on Cultural Development.

First publication in the United States, 1999

Formac Publishing Company Limited acknowledges the support of the Canada Council and the Nova Scotia Department of Education and Culture in the development of writing and publishing in Canada.

---

**Canadian Cataloguing in Publiscation Data**

Hutchins, H.J. (Hazel J.)

  Robyn's want ad

  (First novels. The new series)

ISBN 0-88780-458-6 (pbk.) — ISBN 0-88780-459-4 (bound)

I. Cathcart, Yvonne. II. Title. III. Series.

PS8565.U826R62 1998   jC813'.54 C98-950220-1

PZ7.H9612Ro 1998

---

Formac Publishing
Limited
5502 Atlantic Street
Halifax, NS B3H 1G4

Distributed in the U.S. by:
Orca Book Publishers
P.O. Box 468 Custer, WA
U.S.A. 98240-0468

Printed and bound in Canada

# Table of Contents

# 1
## Part-time Brother

I get fed up with being an only child. That's why I put the ad in the weekly newspaper.

> *Wanted–Older Brother.*
> *Good at math.*
> *Wicked on a skateboard.*
> Must share TV time.
> *Apply to Robyn, #402, Hillside Apartments*

My mom was pretty surprised when she saw it.

"The paper is giving free want ads this month," I explained.

"An ad for a brother?" asked my mom, shaking her head. "Robyn, no one is going to apply. And if they did, who knows what sort of person they might be."

Just then the doorbell rang. My mom answered the door. I couldn't see who it was, but I could hear.

"Is this the right place for the ad?" asked a boy's voice.

"Yes," began my mom, "but..."

"Don't worry," said the voice. "I've got a real home. I only want to apply part-time. I won't eat all your food or anything."

Perfect, I thought.

"But it's too dangerous for someone your age to be answering ads in the paper," said my mom.

"Robyn's kind of weird, but she's not dangerous," said the voice.

Not so perfect. I stuck my head around the door. There stood Ari Grady.

Ari Grady is in my class at school. He belongs to a gang that my friend Marie and I call "The Three G's." We'd like to call them "The Three Twerps" but our teachers won't let us.

"I take it you two know each other,"said my mom.

We know each other all right but I think it's against the law to turn down someone just because he's a twerp.

"Interviews are being held in the office," I said.

I led the way to the spare room.

# 2
## Piano Lessons

"Nice room," said Ari.

"Thanks," I said.

"Nice apartment," said Ari.

"Thanks," I said.

"Don't tell anyone I came here," said Ari.

That was the best thing I'd heard yet.

"Right," I said. "Besides, you can't apply. The ad says older brother."

"I spent two years in grade one," said Ari.

Just my luck.

"But I'm good at math," said Ari.

Strange, but true.

"And I'm wicked on a skate-board, but mine is broken," he said. "Can I start right now?"

"No," I said. "You're not suit-able."

I thought that sounded pretty good–"not suitable."

"Aw, come on, Robyn," said Ari. "It'll only take five min-utes. I'll be your brother and you can teach me something—like how to play the piano. And then I'll be outta here."

I began to smell a rat.

"What does piano have to do with this?" I asked.

"Everyone knows you play piano. I just need a quick lesson," said Ari.

"No," I said.

He turned away and took something from his pocket. When he turned back, he had a couple of dollars in his hand. The money was interesting, but the purple envelope he was sneaking back into his pocket was more interesting.

"I can even pay you," he said.

It all came clear. Mrs. Janvier is the music teacher in our area. When kids sign up with her, she gives them purple envelopes to bring their lesson money in every week. It's a lot more than a couple of dollars.

"You're stealing!" I told Ari. "Your mom is paying for real piano lessons, but you want me to give them to you cheap. You're going to keep the rest of the money! That's awful!"

Ari turned red in the face. I thought he'd get mad or start making excuses, but he didn't. All he did was turn red.

"I'm not stealing," he said. "That's all I'm telling you. You're the one who's always bragging about how great you are on the piano. I bet you're not great at all. I bet you couldn't teach someone to play the piano, no matter what."

I hate it when someone says I can't do something—especially when I know perfectly well I can.

# 3
# Ari's Secret

I taught Ari how to play the C scale, just to prove I know about playing the piano. I also taught him a song with five notes. It's an easy song to remember if you say the words as you do it:

"C D E and C B A are the notes you're playing."

It really did take only five minutes. I didn't take his money.

"I'm not going to be part of anyone stealing," I told him.

Ari glared at me, but he didn't answer.

"Do you think I've learned enough to fool my mom?" he asked, instead.

"Sure," I said. "But Mrs. Janvier will rat on you so you'll still get in trouble."

"I told Mrs. Janvier I'm not starting lessons for a couple of weeks," said Ari. "See you next time!"

With that he was gone.

A couple of weeks? See you next time? I didn't want to be stuck with Ari every Saturday for the rest of my life! Especially if he was stealing! Was he taking his Mom's money or wasn't he?

I raced out of the apartment and down the stairs. I caught him at the front door.

"What are you going to do with the money in the envelope?" I asked.

"I'm saving it," said Ari.

He pushed out the door. I followed him.

"What are you saving it for?" I asked.

"Go away," said Ari.

"If you don't tell me I'll follow you home," I said.

Ari glared at me. He glared so hard a lady across the street stopped to look at us. Ari turned red again. He walked around the next corner. I followed him.

"All right," he said. "I'll tell you, but don't you go blabbing about it. It's no big deal. My mom really needs some new gloves. I'm saving to buy her a pair for her birthday."

It had to be the truth. It was too wild to be a lie.

# 4
# All the World Reads
# Want Ads

"How did things work out with Ari?" asked my mom.

"He doesn't want a sister," I said. "He wants a piano teacher."

I didn't tell her about the gloves. I know what it's like when your family doesn't have a lot of money and you want to buy something special for your mom. Mom and I don't have a lot of money ourselves.

She gave me a hug. She didn't like my want ad, but at least she understood about me wanting a

brother. My best friend Marie didn't understand at all.

"You're nuts," said Marie when she phoned later. "Older brothers are a pain! Any ad about older brothers should read 'For Sale'."

Marie has two older brothers.

"How do you know about the ad?" I asked.

"My mom saw it. She thought it was cute."

Cute! I didn't want it to be cute! And I didn't want everyone in the world to know I was looking for a brother.

Why hadn't I thought of that? Why hadn't I realized that it wasn't just strangers—like the perfect older brother—who read the paper. If Marie's mom and Ari had seen it, other kids I know might have seen or heard about it too–a lot of other kids. Why do I do these things!

I phoned the newspaper office. I stopped next week's ad before I became the laughing stock of the school.

I found out on Monday that it was already too late.

# 5
## Marie's Advice

"Hey Robyn—that was a real dumb ad in the paper!"

"Hey Robyn—you'd have to pay someone a million dollars to be your brother!"

"Hey Robyn—I hear you used to have a brother but you scared him off!"

The last comment was from smart aleck Grant Smith. He's the leader of the Three G's. He would have been pretty surprised to know his buddy Ari had applied for the job.

But I didn't tell. Ari was standing behind Grant shaking

his head like mad. Besides, I'd seen Ari's mother at a bus stop on my way to school that morning. She really did need new gloves. Her old ones were a horrible green and purple pair. They had mended bits and fuzzy strings falling off them.

I turned my back on Grant Smith and the others.

"If I had a big brother, a really big brother, they wouldn't be teasing me," I told my friend Marie. "They'd be running away."

"It's not worth it," said Marie. "I've told you about brothers. They're messy. They watch dumb stuff on TV. They run around the house yelling and wrestling and throwing footballs."

It sounded great to me. Marie was really getting me down.

"Don't you even like your brothers?" I asked her.

"Sure I like them," she said. "I just don't want to live with them all the time. I'd like them to be part-time brothers, kind of like cousins." Cousins! Sometimes Marie is a genius.

# 6
## Long-distance Brother

As soon as I got home from school I phoned my cousin Tim. He lives in the mountains. It was a long-distance phone call, but I only planned to talk for a minute or two.

"Tim? It's Robyn."

"Robyn? Hey—neat. How are ya?"

"Terrible," I said. "I need an older brother. Ask your mom if you can move to the city. It's nice here. Lots to do. Great people. Be here by noon tomorrow."

"What?"

It felt great to ask him, but I knew in my heart it wasn't going to happen.

"Never mind," I said. "I just phoned to say hi. How are the mountains? Seen any bears lately?"

"Everything's great," said Tim. "I've got lots to tell you."

Tim tells great stories. He knows how to listen too. I didn't exactly tell him what was wrong, but he cheered me up. By the time Mom came home, Tim and I were telling jokes.

"Why did the duck stand in the middle of the road?"

"I don't know."

"To prove he wasn't chicken."

Mom smiled and went out to the kitchen to make supper. When I hung up about half an

hour later I went out to help her.

"That sounded like a fun phone call," said my mom. "Who was it, Robyn?"

"Tim," I said.

"Tim?" My mom looked at me funny. "Your cousin Tim?"

"Yeah, he's almost as good as a brother. We're going to phone each other every day and make up jokes."

"Robyn," said my mom. I could tell she was pretty upset, but she was trying not to yell. "Robyn, if you and Tim tell jokes every day long-distance on the phone, we won't be able to afford supper. Or lunch. Or even breakfast."

I looked at the spaghetti cooking in the pot. I definitely like supper.

"Does it really cost that much?"

"Yes!" said my mom.

"We'll write letters instead," I said.

But it wouldn't be the same.

# 7
## Ari's Routine

Saturday morning, same time as last week, Ari turned up at the door.

"Hey, sis!" he said and walked in.

"I'm only doing this because of your mother," I said. "Sit down. Be quiet. Play your scales."

He played his scales. He played them perfectly. I frowned. I was hoping he'd be terrible, then I could refuse to teach him because he wasn't practising. That's what Mrs. Janvier does.

"Play your piece," I said.

He played his piece. He played it slow. He played it fast. He played it with a boogie beat.

I looked at him hard. I didn't know twerps could learn to play the piano.

I gave him a scale with a sharp. A sharp is a black note—the scales with black notes are harder. I gave him a piece with two hands at once. That's harder too. He learned both in no time.

"How can you learn to play so quickly?" I asked.

Ari shrugged.

"I just can," he said. "I fool around on our piano at home. That's why my mom wants me to take lessons. Now what?"

"Now you go home," I said.

"I can't," he said. "Last time Mom wondered why I was back so soon."

"That's not my problem," I said.

"We could watch TV," he said.

"I'm saving my TV time until later," I said. "I only get one hour."

One of the reasons I wanted a brother was so that he'd get his own hour of TV and I could watch it too.

"I could help you with your math," he said.

"I've done it," I said. "It was easier this week."

"We could fool around on your skateboard," he said.

"I don't have one," I said. Another reason I'd wanted a brother.

"We could just sit around," he said.

And that's what we did.

Ari was the most boring pretend brother I've ever met.

# 8
# Mr. Kelly's Surprise

It was weird. All that week it seemed like everyone in the whole world had exactly what I didn't have.

There were brothers and sisters all over the TV screen. They were joking, kidding and having a great time.

There was a book at school about a girl finding her long lost brother. He was a famous rock star and she became a famous rock star too.

And on Wednesday, Marie was given a really good secondhand skateboard by—you guessed it—her brother.

It was depressing.

Thursday night I went over to help Mr. Kelly with the twins. I help him every Thursday while Mrs. Kelly has a night out.

"You're awfully quiet tonight, Robyn," said Mr. Kelly. "Does it have something to do with your ad in the paper?"

That ad was going to bug me forever.

"Kind of," I said.

"If it helps, you're like a sister to the twins," said Mr. Kelly.

The twins were lying on the carpet. I was handing them toys. I smiled at them.

"They're great," I said. "It's just ... right now, they're pretty little."

"And you're looking for some-one older," said Mr. Kelly.

"An older brother would make things happen around our place—you know, fun things," I said. "I don't mean to hurt the twins' feelings."

They were both grinning up at me. I think I was pretty safe.

"That's odd," said Mr. Kelly. "I can understand that you might want brothers or sisters once in a while, but as for making things happen—I always think you're good at that yourself."

"You do?" I asked.

"Mmm," said Mr. Kelly. "In fact I found some things in a box the other day—things from when I was a kid. Right away they made me think of you."

Mr. Kelly brought out the box. He looked almost like a kid himself as he opened it.

There was a jar marked Cold Cream. When you unscrewed the lid a paper snake came exploding out and scared a person half to death.

There were creepy plastic flies in real-looking plastic ice cubes.

And there was a whoopie cushion.

"Wow," I said.

"I was hoping you might feel that way," said Mr. Kelly.

# 9
# Green and Purple

I tried out the snake on Marie. She almost hit the roof. She liked it so much she took it to try on her brothers.

I tried the ice cube flies on my mom. She screamed and threw her glass of ice water in the air. After that I tried it on Mrs. Kelly and the caretaker. Things were definitely picking up around our place.

But I saved the whoopie cushion for Saturday. That Saturday I blew up the whoopie cushion and put it in the piano bench, so the lid was propped open, just a

little. When Ari sat down for his lesson, the sound was terrific.

You should have seen the look on his face. He thought it was great. He thought it was hilarious. We both laughed until we cried.

"I knew something crazy would happen around here sooner or later," said Ari.

He sounded happy about it. He blew up the cushion and made rude noises while he played the piano. He even did it to the beat. We laughed until our stomachs hurt.

That's when the doorbell rang. My mom answered it. We could hear a lady's voice say something about "Music lessons" and "A neighbour happened to see..." From the look on Ari's face, I knew it was his mother's voice. A moment later, both moms came into the living room.

"Oh, Ari," said his mom when she saw him sitting there.

Moms can make you feel awful with just two words.

"Give her the gloves," I whispered in Ari's ear.

He'd bought them at a store that morning, on the way over to my place. The bag was beside the piano.

"Her birthday's not until tomorrow," Ari whispered back.

"Close enough," I said.

Ari held the bag out to his mother. She looked at it, puzzled.

"Ari didn't steal his lesson money or anything Mrs. Grady," I said. "He just kind of made it stretch further. And he really has been learning piano–in fact he's great."

I couldn't read the look on Mrs. Grady's face as she took the bag. She looked inside and slowly removed a pair of sleek, black leather gloves. She took a little step backward and sat on the sofa.

"And here's the change," said Ari. He dropped it in her lap. "Happy Birthday."

I still couldn't figure out the look on Mrs. Grady's face.

"Now you won't have to wear green and purple gloves with loose strings and holes in them," I said, trying to help things along.

Mrs. Grady took her old gloves from her coat pocket. She looked at them and shook her head.

"Do you know why I wear these, Robyn?" she asked.

I thought I knew. I thought it was because she couldn't afford a new pair. From the way she looked up at us, however, I wasn't sure any more.

"I wear them because Ari chose them for me when he was three," said Mrs. Grady. "Green and purple. Only green and purple would do."

The room was very, very quiet.

"We could take them back and get green and purple," said Ari.

Even though you could tell by the look on her face that Mrs. Grady was happy, her eyes were all full of tears. Mothers are crazy.

"My new gloves are beautiful Ari," she said. "I like them just the way they are."

# 10
# Robyn on her Own with Friends

Ari doesn't come to my house for piano lessons on Saturdays anymore. He goes to Mrs. Janvier for real lessons. She loves him. He's a natural.

But sometimes, on his way home, he drops in at my place. Maybe he just forgets where he's going. Or maybe he likes the idea that sometimes crazy things happen at my place.

He teaches me how to play my songs to a boogie beat. I teach him jokes from my cousin Tim. After that we make up our own

neat rules for playing cards or board games, or we blow up the whoopie cushion.

If it gets late, Mom lets Ari watch his favourite TV show. I get to watch it too, without using up my own ration. And if I do come up with an idea that's kind of crazy—I save it until Ari's around.

At school, of course, Marie and I still think of Ari as one of the Three G's gang—but we both agree that he's less annoying than the other two.

Is he my adopted brother? No, he's just Ari. That's OK. I don't really need a brother—I can make fun things happen perfectly well on my own.

But I can always use a friend.

## About the Author...

HAZEL HUTCHINS lives in Canmore, Alberta. She has written 16 books for children as well as *Robyn's Want Ad* and *Shoot for the Moon, Robyn*. She has been awarded the Writers Guild of Alberta Award for Children's Literature and has been nominated for the Governor General's and Mr. Christie awards.

## About the Illustrator...

YVONNE CATHCART is an illustrator living in Toronto with her husband and son. She has illustrated many children's books, as well as *Robyn's Want Ad* and *Shoot for the Moon, Robyn*, and also paints and makes animal sculptures and puppets.

# Another story about Robyn...

### • *Shoot for the Moon, Robyn*
by Hazel Hutchins/Illustrated by
Yvonne Cathcart

When the teacher asks her to sing for the
class, Robyn knows it's her chance to be
the world's best singer. Should she perform
like Celine Dion, or do *My Bonnie Lies
Over the Ocean*, or the matchmaker song?
It's hard to decide, even for the world's
best singer — and the three boys who
throw spitballs don't make it any easier.

# Meet five other great kids in the New First Novels Series...

# Meet Morgan in

### • *Morgan and the Money*
by Ted Staunton/Illustrated by Bill Slavin

When money for the class trip goes
missing, Morgan wonders who to tell
about seeing Aldeen Hummel, the Godzilla
of Grade 3, at the teacher's desk with
the envelope. Morgan only wants to do
the right thing, but it's hard to know if not

telling all the truth would be the same as telling a lie.

### • *Morgan Makes Magic*
by Ted Staunton/Illustrated by Bill Slavin
When he's in a tight spot, Morgan tells stories — and most of them stretch the truth, to say the least. But when he tells kids at his new school he can do magic tricks, he really gets in trouble — most of all with the dreaded Aldeen Hummel!

# Meet Jan in
### • *Jan and Patch*
by Monica Hughes/Illustrated by Carlos Freire
Jan wants a puppy so badly that she would do just about anything to get one. But her mother and her gramma won't allow one in the house. So when Jan and her friend Sarah meet a puppy at the pet store, they know they have to find a creative way to make him Jan's.

### • *Jan's Big Bang*
by Monica Hughes/Illustrated by Carlos Freire
Taking part in the Science Fair is a big deal for Grade 3 kids, but Jan and her best friend Sarah are ready for the challenge. Still, finding a safe project isn't easy, and the girls

discover that getting ready for the fair can cause a whole lot of trouble.

# Meet Lilly in

## • *Lilly's Good Deed*
by Brenda Bellingham/Illustrated by Kathy Kaulbach

Lilly can't stand Theresa Green. Now she is living on Lilly's street and making trouble. First, Lilly's friend Minna gets hurt because of Theresa's clumsiness, then Lilly is hurled off her bike when Theresa gets in the way. But when they have to work together to save the life of a kitten, Lilly has a change of heart.

## • *Lilly to the Rescue*
by Brenda Bellingham/Illustrated by Kathy Kaulbach

Bossy-boots! That's what kids at school start calling Lilly when she gives a lot of advice that's not wanted. Lilly can't help telling people what to do — but how can she keep any of her friends if she always knows better?

# Meet Carrie in

### • *Carrie's Crowd*
by Lesley Choyce/Illustrated by Mark Thurman

Carrie wants to be part of the cool crowd. Becoming friends with them means getting a new image for herself but it also means ignoring her old friends. That's when Carrie starts to see that there are friends, and then there are good friends.

### • *Go For It, Carrie*
by Lesley Choyce/Illustrated by Mark Thurman

More than anything else, Carrie wants to roller-blade. Her big brother and his friend just laugh at her. But Carrie knows she can do it if she just keeps trying. As her friend Gregory tells her, "You can do it, Carrie. Go for it!"

# Meet Duff in

### • *Duff the Giant Killer*
by Budge Wilson/Illustrated by Kim LaFave

Getting over the chicken pox can be boring, but Duff and Simon find a great way to enjoy themselves — acting out one of their favourite stories, *Jack the Giant Killer*, in the park. In fact, they do it so well the police get into the act.

# Look for these First Novels!

• *About Arthur*
Arthur Throws a Tantrum
Arthur's Dad
Arthur's Problem Puppy

• *About Fred*
Fred and the Flood
Fred and the Stinky Cheese
Fred's Dream Cat

• *About the Loonies*
Loonie Summer
The Loonies Arrive

• *About Maddie*
Maddie in Trouble
Maddie in Hospital
Maddie Goes to Paris
Maddie in Danger
Maddie in Goal
Maddie Wants Music
That's Enough Maddie!

• *About Mikey*
Mikey Mite's Best Present
Good For You, Mikey Mite!
Mikey Mite Goes to School
Mikey Mite's Big Problem

• *About Mooch*
Mooch Forever
Hang On, Mooch!
Mooch Gets Jealous
Mooch and Me

• *About the Swank Twins*
The Swank Prank
Swank Talk

• *About Max*
Max the Superhero

• *About Will*
Will and His World

---

**Formac Publishing Company Limited**
5502 Atlantic Street, Halifax, Nova Scotia B3H 1G4
Orders: 1-800-565-1975  Fax: (902) 425-0166